RAJA RASALU

A FOLK-TALE OF PUNJAB

GOLU KUMAR

Contents

ONE

Birth of Raja Rasâlu.

Once there lived a great Raja, whose name was Sâlbâhan, and he had two Queens. Now the elder, by name Queen Achhrâ, had a fair young son called Prince Pûran; but the younger, by name Lonâ, though she wept and prayed at many a shrine, had never a child to gladden her eyes. So, being a bad, deceitful woman, envy and rage took possession of her heart, and she so poisoned Raja Sâlbâhan's mind against his son, young Pûran, that just as the Prince was growing to manhood, his father became madly jealous of him, and in a fit of anger ordered his hands and feet to be cut off. Not content even with this cruelty, Raja Sâlbâhan had the poor young man thrown into a deep well. Nevertheless, Pûran did not die, as no doubt, the enraged father hoped and expected; for God preserved the innocent Prince, so that he lived on, miraculously, at the bottom of the well, until, years after, the great and holy Guru Goraknâth came to the place, and finding Prince Pûran still alive, not only released him from his dreadful prison but, by the power of magic, restored his hands and feet. Then Pûran, in gratitude for this great boon, became a _faqîr_, and placing the sacred earrings in his ears, followed Goraknâth as a disciple, and was called Pûran Bhagat.

But as time went by, his heart yearned to see his mother's face, so Guru Goraknâth gave him leave to visit his native town, and Pûran Bhagat journeyed thither and took up his abode in a large walled garden, where he had often played as a child. And, lo! he found it neglected and barren so that his heart became sad when he saw the broken watercourses and the withered trees. Then he sprinkled the dry ground with water from his drinking vessel and prayed that all might become green again. And, lo! even as he prayed, the trees shot forth leaves, the grass grew, the flowers bloomed, and all was as it had once been.

The news of this marvelous thing spread fast through the city, and all the world went out to see the holy man who had performed the wonder. Even the Raja Sâlbâhan and his two Queens heard of it in the palace, and they too went to the garden to see it with their own eyes. But Pûran Bhagat's mother, Queen Achhrâ, had wept so long for her darling, that the tears had blinded her eyes, and so she went, not to see, but to ask the wonder-working _faqîr_ to restore her sight. Therefore, little knowing from whom she asked the boon, she fell on the ground before Pûran Bhagat, begging him to cure her; and, lo! almost before she asked, it was done, and she saw plainly.

Then deceitful Queen Lonâ, who all these years had been longing vainly for a son when she saw what mighty power the unknown _faqîr_ possessed, fell on the ground also, and begged for an heir to gladden the heart of Raja Sâlbâhan.

Then Pûran Bhagat spoke, and his voice was stern,--'Raja Sâlbâhan already has a son. Where is he? What have you done with him? Speak the truth, Queen Lonâ, if you would find favor with God!'

Then the woman's great longing for a son conquered her pride, and though her husband stood by, she humbled herself before the _faqîr_ and told the truth,--how she had deceived the father and destroyed the son.

Then Pûran Bhagat rose to his feet, stretched out his hands towards her, and a smile was on his face, as he said softly, 'Even so, Queen Lonâ! even so! And behold! _I_ am Prince Pûran, whom you destroyed and God delivered! I have a message for you. Your fault is forgiven, but not forgotten; you shall indeed bear a son, who shall be brave and good, yet will he cause you to weep tears as bitter as those my mother wept for me. So! take this grain of rice; eat it, and you shall bear a son that will be no son to you, for even as I was reft from my mother's eyes, so will he be reft from yours. Go in peace; your fault is forgiven, but not forgotten!'

Queen Lonâ returned to the palace, and when the time for the birth of the promised son drew nigh, she inquired of three Jôgis who came begging to her gate, what the child's fate would be, and the youngest of them answered and said, 'O Queen, the child will be a boy, and he will live to be a great man. But for twelve years you must not look upon his face, for if either you or his father see it before the twelve years are past, you will surely die! This is what you must do,--as soon as the child is born you must send him away to a cellar underneath the ground, and never let him see the light of day for twelve years. After they are over, he may come forth, bathe in the river, put on new clothes, and visit you. His name shall be Raja Rasâlu, and he shall be known far and wide.' So, when a fair young Prince was in due time born into the world, his parents hid him away in an underground palace, with nurses, servants, and everything else a King's son might desire. And with him, they sent a young colt, born the same day, and a sword, a spear, and a shield, against the day when Raja Rasâlu should go forth into the world. So there the child lived, playing with his colt, and talking to his parrot, while the nurses taught him all things needful for a King's son to know.

THE WAY RAJA RASLU ENTERED THE WORLD

Young Rasâlu lived on, far from the light of day, for eleven long years, growing tall and strong, yet contented to remain to play with his colt and talk to his parrot; but when the twelfth year began, the lad's heart leaped up with desire for change, and he loved to listen to the sounds of life which came to him in his palace-prison from the outside world.

'I must go and see where the voices come from!' he said; and when his nurses told him he must not go for one year more, he only laughed aloud, saying, 'Nay! I stay no longer here for any man!'

Then he saddled his horse Bhaunr Irâqi, put on his shining armor, and rode forth into the world; but--mindful of what his nurses had often told him--when he came to the river, he dismounted, and going into the water, washed himself and his clothes.

Then, clean of raiment, fair of face, and brave of heart, he rode on his way until he reached his father's city. There he sat down to rest a while by a well, where the women were drawing water in earthen pitchers. Now, as they passed him, their full pitchers poised upon their heads, the gay young Prince flung stones at the earthen vessels and broke them all. Then the women, drenched with water, went weeping and wailing to the palace, complaining to the King that a mighty young Prince in shining armor, with a parrot on his wrist and a gallant steed beside him, sat by the well, and broke their pitchers.

Now, as soon as Raja Sâlbâhan heard this, he guessed at once that it was Prince Rasâlu come forth before the time, and, mindful of the Jôgis' words that he would die if he looked on his son's face before twelve years were passed, he did not dare to send his guards to seize the offender and bring him to be judged. So he bade the women be comforted, and for the future take pitchers of iron and brass, and gave new ones from his treasury to those who did not possess any of their own.

But when Prince Rasâlu saw the women returning to the well with pitchers of iron and brass, he laughed to himself and drew his mighty bow till the sharp-pointed arrows pierced the metal vessels as though they had been clay.

Yet still, the King did not send for him, and so he mounted his steed and set off in the pride of his youth and strength to the palace. He strode into the audience hall, where his father sat trembling, and saluted him with all reverence; but Raja Sâlbâhan, in fear of his life, turned his back hastily and said never a word in reply.

Then Prince Rasâlu called scornfully to him across the hall--

'I came to greet thee, King, and not to harm thee!
What have I done that thou shouldst turn away?
Sceptre and empire have no power to charm me--
I go to seek a worthier prize than they!'

Then he strode out of the hall, full of bitterness and anger; but, as he passed under the palace windows, he heard his mother weeping, and the sound softened his heart so that his wrath died down, and great loneliness fell upon him because he was spurned by both father and mother. So he cried sorrowfully--

'O heart crowned with grief, hast thou naught
But tears for thy son?
Art mother of mine? Give one thought
To my life just begun!'

And Queen Lonâ answered through her tears--

'Yea! mother am I, though I weep,
So hold this word sure,--
Go, reign king of all men, but keep
Thy heart good and pure!'

So Raja Rasâlu was comforted and began to make ready for fortune. He took with him his horse Bhaunr Irâqi, and his parrot, both of whom had lived with him since he was born; and besides these tried and trusted friends he had two others--a carpenter lad, and a goldsmith lad, who was determined to follow the Prince till death.

So they made a goodly company, and Queen Lona, when she saw them going, watched them from her window till she saw nothing but a cloud of dust on the horizon; then she bowed her head on her hands and wept, saying--

'O son who ne'er gladdened my eyes,
Let the cloud of thy going arise,
Dim the sunlight and darken the day;
For the mother whose son is away
Is as dust!'

HOW THE FRIENDS OF RAJA RASLU LEFT HIM.

Now, on the first day, Raja Rasâlu journeyed far, until he came to a lonely forest, where he halted for the night. And seeing it was a desolate place, and the night dark, he determined to set a watch. So he divided the time into three watches, and the carpenter took the first, the goldsmith the second, and Raja Rasâlu the third.

Then the goldsmith lad spread a couch of clean grass for his master, and fearing lest the Prince's heart should sink at the change from his former luxurious life, he said these words of encouragement--

'Cradled till now on softest down,
The grass is thy couch tonight;
Yet grieve not thou if Fortune frown--

Brave hearts heed not her slight!'

Now, when Raja Rasâlu and the goldsmith's son slept, a snake came out of a thicket hard by and crept towards the sleepers.

'Who are you?' quoth the carpenter lad, 'and why do you come hither?'

'I have destroyed all things within twelve miles!' returned the serpent. 'Who is _you_ that have dared to come hither?

Then the snake attacked the carpenter, and they fought until the snake was killed, when the carpenter hid the dead body under his shield, and said nothing of the adventure to his comrades, lest he should alarm them, for, like the goldsmith, he thought the Prince might be discouraged.

Now, when it came to Raja Rasâlu's turn to keep watch, a dreadful unspeakable horror came out of the thicket. Nevertheless, Rasâlu went up to it boldly, and cried aloud, 'Who are you? and what brings you here?'

Then the awful unspeakable horror replied, 'I have killed everything for thrice twelve miles around! Who are _you_ that dare come hither?'

Whereupon Rasâlu drew his mighty bow, and pierced the horror with an arrow, so that it fled into a cave, whither the Prince followed it. And they fought long and fiercely, till at last the horror died, and Rasâlu returned to watch in peace.

Now, when morning broke, Raja Rasâlu called his sleeping servants, and the carpenter showed with pride the body of the serpent he had killed.

'Tis but a small snake!' quoth the Raja. 'Come and see what I killed in the cave!'

And, behold! when the goldsmith lad and the carpenter lad saw the awful, dreadful, unspeakable horror Raja

Rasâlu had slain, they were exceedingly afraid, and falling on their knees, begged to be allowed to return to the city, saying, 'O mighty Rasâlu, you are a Raja and a hero! You can fight such horrors; we are but ordinary folk, and if we follow you we shall surely be killed. Such things are naught to you, but they are death to us. Let us go!'

Then Rasâlu looked at them sorrowfully, and bade them do as they wished, saying--

'Aloes linger long before they flower:
Gracious rain too soon is overpast:
Youth and strength are with us but an hour:
All glad life must end in death at last!

But the king reigns king without the consent of the courtier;
Rulers may rule, though none heed their command.
Heaven-crown'd heads stoop not, but rise the haughtier,
Alone and houseless in a stranger's land!'

So his friends forsook him, and Rasâlu journeyed on alone.

DUE TO RAJA RASUL, THE GIANTS WERE KILLED.

Now, after a time, Raja Rasâlu arrived at Nila city, and as he entered the town he saw an old woman making unleavened bread, and as she made it she sometimes wept and sometimes laughed; so Rasâlu asked her why she wept and laughed, but she answered sadly, as she kneaded her cakes, 'Why do you ask? What will you gain by it?'

'Nay, mother!' replied Rasâlu, 'if you tell me the truth, one of us must benefit by it.'

And when the old woman looked in Rasâlu's face she saw that it was kind, so she opened her heart to him, saying, with tears, 'O stranger, I had seven fair sons, and now I have but one left, for six of them have been killed by a dreadful giant who comes every day to this city to receive tribute from us,--every day a fair young man, a buffalo, and a basket of cakes! Six of my sons have gone, and now today it has once more fallen to my lot to provide the tribute; and my boy, my darling, my youngest, must meet the fate of his brothers. Therefore I weep!'

Then Rasâlu was moved to pity and said--

'Fond, foolish mother! cease these tears--
Keep thou thy son. I fear nor death nor life,
Seeking my fortune everywhere in strife.
My head for his I give!--so calm your fears.'

Still, the old woman shook her head doubtfully, saying, 'Fair words, fair words! but who will risk his life for another?'

Then Rasâlu smiled at her, and dismounting from his gallant steed, Bhaunr Irâqi, he sat down carelessly to rest, as if indeed he were a son of the house, and said, 'Fear not, mother! I give you my word of honor that I will risk my life to save your son.'

Just then the high officials of the city, whose duty it was to claim the giant's tribute, appeared in sight, and the old woman fell a-weeping once more, saying--

'O Prince, with the gallant gray steed and the
turban bound high
O'er thy fair bearded face; keep thy word, my
oppressor draws nigh!'

Then Raja Rasâlu rose in his shining armor and haughtily bade the guards stand aside.

'Fair words!' replied the chief officer; 'but if this woman does not send the tribute at once, the giants will come and disturb the whole city. Her son must go!'

'I go in his stead!' quoth Rasâlu more haughtily still. 'Stand back, and let me pass!'

Then, despite their denials, he mounted his horse, and taking the basket of cakes and the buffalo, he set off to find the giant, bidding the buffalo to show him the shortest road.

Now, as he came near the giants' house, he met one of them carrying a huge skinful of water. No sooner did the water-carrier giant see Raja Rasâlu riding along on his horse Bhaunr Irâqi and leading the buffalo, than he said to himself, 'Oho! we have a horse extra today! I think I will eat it myself before my brothers see it!'

Then he reached out his hand, but Rasâlu drew his sharp sword and smote the giant's hand off at a blow so that he fled from him in great fear.

Now, as he fled, he met his sister the giantess, who called out to him, 'Brother, whither away so fast?'

And the giant answered in haste, 'Raja Rasâlu has come at last, and see!--he has cut off my hand with one blow of his sword!'

Then the giantess, overcome with fear, fled with her brother, and as they fled they called aloud--

'Fly! brethren, fly!
Take the nearest path;
The fire burns high
That will scorch up our dearest!
Life's joys we have seen:
East and west we must wander!
What has been, has been;
Quick! some remedy ponder.'

Then all the giants turned and fled to their astrologer brother, and bade him look in his books to see if Raja Rasâlu were born into the world. And when they heard that he was, they prepared to fly east and west; but even as they turned, Raja Rasâlu rode up on Bhaunr Irâqi, and challenged them to fight, saying, 'Come forth, for I am Rasâlu, son of Raja

Sâlbâhan, and born enemy of the giants!'

Then one of the giants tried to brazen it out, saying, 'I have eaten many Rasâlus like you! When the real man comes, his horse's heel-ropes will bind us and his sword cut us up of their own accord!'

Then Raja Rasâlu loosed his heel-ropes, and dropped his sword upon the ground, and, lo! the heel-ropes bound the giants, and the sword cut them in pieces.

Still, seven giants who were left tried to brazen it out, saying, 'Aha! We have eaten many Rasâlus like you! When the real man comes, his arrow will pierce seven girdles placed one behind the other.'

So they took seven iron girdles for baking bread, and placed them one behind the other, as a shield, and behind them stood the seven giants, who were their brothers, and, lo! when Raja Rasâlu twanged his mighty bow, the arrow pierced through the seven girdles, and spitted the seven giants in a row!

But the giantess, their sister, escaped, and fled to a cave in the Gandgari mountains. Then Raja Rasâlu had a statue made in His likeness, and clad it in shining armor, with sword and spear and shield. And he placed it as a sentinel at the entrance of the cave, so that the giantess dared not come forth, but starved to death inside.

So this is how he killed the giants.

RAJA RASLU'S JOGI TRANSITION.

Then, after a time, Rasâlu went to Hodinagari. And when he reached the house of the beautiful far-famed Queen Sundrân, he saw an old Jôgi sitting at the gate, by the side of his sacred fire.

'Wherefore do you sit there, father?' asked Raja Rasâlu.

'My son,' returned the Jôgi, 'for two-and-twenty years have I waited thus to see the beautiful Sundrân, yet have I never seen her!'

'Make me your pupil,' quoth Rasâlu, 'and I will wait too.'

'You work miracles already, my son,' said the Jôgi; 'so where is the use of your becoming one of us?'

Nevertheless, Raja Rasâlu would not be denied, so the Jôgi bored his ears and put in the sacred earrings. Then the new disciple put aside his shining armor, and sat by the fire in a Jôgi's loin-cloth, waiting to see Queen Sundrân.

Then, at night, the old Jôgi went and begged alms from four houses, and half of what he got he gave to Rasâlu, and a half he ate himself. Now Raja Rasâlu, being a very holy man, and a hero besides, did not care for food and was well content with his half share, but the Jôgi felt starved.

The next day the same thing happened, and still, Rasâlu sat by the fire waiting to see the beautiful Queen Sundrân.

Then the Jôgi lost patience, and said, 'O my disciple, I made you a pupil so that you might beg, and feed me, and behold, it is I who have to starve to feed you!'

'You gave no orders!' quoth Rasâlu, laughing. 'How can a disciple beg without his master's leave?'

'I order you now!' returned the Jôgi. 'Go and beg enough for you and me.'

So Raja Rasâlu rose, and stood at the gate of Queen Sundrân's palace, in his Jôgi's dress, and sang,

'_Alakh!_ at thy threshold I stand,
Drawn from far by the name of thy charms;
Fair Sundrân, with a generous hand,
Give the earring-decked Jôgi an alms!'

Now when Queen Sundrân, from within, heard Rasâlu's voice, its sweetness pierced her heart, so that she immediately sent out alms by the hand of her maid-servant. But when the maiden came to the gate, and saw the exceeding beauty of Rasâlu, standing outside, fair in face and form, she fainted away, dropping the alms upon the ground.

Then once more Rasâlu sang, and again his voice fell sweetly on Queen Sundrân's ears so that she sent out more alms by the hand of another maiden. But she also fainted away at the sight of Rasâlu's marvelous beauty.

Then Queen Sundrân rose and came forth herself, fair and stately. She chid the maidens, gathered up the broken alms, and setting the food aside, filled the plate with jewels and put it herself into Rasâlu's hands, saying proudly--

'Since when have the earrings been thine?
Since when were thou made a _faqîr_?
What arrow from Love's bow has struck thee?
What seekest thou here?
Do you beg of all women you see,
Or only, fair Jôgi, of me?'

And Rasâlu, in his Jôgi's habit, bent his head towards her, saying softly--

'A day since the earrings were mine,
A day since I turned a _faqîr_;
But yesterday Love's arrow struck me;
I seek nothing here!
I beg naught of others I see,
But only, fair Sundrân, of thee!'

Now, when Rasâlu returned to his master with the plate full of jewels, the old Jôgi was sorely astonished and bade him take them back, and ask for food instead. So Rasâlu returned to the gate and sang--

'_Alakh!_ at thy threshold I stand,
Drawn from far by the fame of thy charms;
Fair Sundrân, with a generous hand,
Give the earring-decked beggar an alms!'

Then Queen Sundrân rose, proud and beautiful, and coming to the gate, said softly--

'No beggar thou! The quiver of thy mouth
Is set with pearly shafts; its bow is red
As rubies are rare. Though ashes hide thy youth,
Thine eyes, thy color, herald it instead!
Deceive me not--pretend no false desire--
But ask the secret alms thou dost require.'

But Rasâlu smiled a scornful smile, saying--

'Fair Queen! what though the quiver of my mouth
Be set with glistening pearls and rubies red?
I trade not jewels, east, west, north, or south;
Take back thy gems, and give me food instead.
Thy gifts are rich and rare, but costly charms
Scarce find fit placing in a Jôgi's alms!'

Then Queen Sundrân took back the jewels and bade the beautiful Jôgi wait an hour till the food was cooked. Nevertheless, she learned no more of him, for he sat by the gate and said never a word. Only when Queen Sundrân gave him a plate piled up with sweets, and looked at him sadly, saying--

'What King's son art thou? and whence dost thou come?
What name hast thou, Jôgi, and where is thy home?'

then Raja Rasâlu, taking the alms, replied--

'I am fair Lona's son; my father's name
Great Sâlbâhan, who reigns at Sialkot.
I am Rasâlu; for thy beauty's fame
These ashes, and the Jôgi's begging note,
To see if thou wert fair as all men say;
Lo! I have seen it, and I go my way!'

Then Rasâlu returned to his master with the sweets, and after that, he went away from the place, for he feared lest the Queen, knowing who he was, might try to keep him prisoner.

And beautiful Sundrân waited for the Jôgi's cry, and when none came, she went forth, proud and stately, to ask the old Jôgi whither his pupil had gone.

Now he, vexed that she should come forth to ask for a stranger, when he had sat at her gates for two-and-twenty years with never a word or sign, answered back, 'My pupil? I was hungry, and I hate him because he did not bring me alms enough.'

'Oh, monster!' cried Queen Sundrân. 'Did I not send thee jewels and sweets? Did not these satisfy thee, that thou must feast on beauty also?'

'I know not,' quoth the Jôgi; 'only this I know--I put the youth on a spit, roasted him, and ate him up. He tasted well!'

'Then roast and eat me too!' cried poor Queen Sundrân, and with the words, she threw herself into the sacred fire and became _sati_ for the love of the beautiful Jôgi Rasâlu.

And he, going thence, though not of her, but fancying he would like to be king a while, snatched the throne from Raja Hari Chand and reigned in his stead.

HOW RAJA RASLU ARRIVED IN KING SARKAP'S CITY.

Now, after he had reigned a while in Hodinagari, Rasâlu gave up his kingdom and started off to play _chaupur_ with King Sarkar. And as he journeyed there came a fierce storm of thunder and lightning, so that he sought shelter, and found none save an old graveyard, where a headless corpse lay upon the ground. So lonesome was it that even the corpse seemed company, and Rasâlu, sitting down beside it, said--

'There is no one here, nor far nor near,
Save this breathless corpse so cold and grim;
Would God he might come to life again,
'Twould be less lonely to talk to him.'

And immediately the headless corpse arose and sat beside Raja Rasâlu. And he, nothing astonished, said to it--

'The storm beats fierce and loud,
The clouds rise thick in the west;
What ails thy grave and thy shroud,
The o corpse, that thou canst not rest?'

Then the headless corpse replied--

'On earth, I was even as thou,
My turban awry like a king,
My head with the highest, I trow,
Having my fun and my fling,
Fighting my foes like a brave,
Living my life with a swing.
And, now I am dead,
Sins, heavy as lead,
Will give me no rest in my grave!'

So the night passed on, dark and dreary, while Rasâlu sat in the graveyard and talked to the headless corpse. Now when morning broke and Rasâlu said he must continue his journey, the headless corpse asked him whither he was going; and when he said. 'to play _chaupur_ with King Sarkap,' the corpse begged him to give up the idea, saying, 'I am King Sarkap's brother, and I know his ways. Every day, before breakfast, he cuts off the heads of two or three men, just to amuse himself. One day no one else was at hand, so he cut off mine, and he will surely cut off yours on some pretense or another. However, if you are determined to go and play _chaupur_ with him, take some of the bones from this graveyard, and make your dice out of them, and then the enchanted dice with which my brother plays will lose their virtue. Otherwise, he will always win.'

So Rasâlu took some of the bones lying about and fashioned them into dice, and these he put into his pocket.

Then, bidding adieu to the headless corpse, he went on his way to play _chaupur_ with the King.

How Raja Rasulu swung the 70 fair maidens, the king's daughters

Now, as Raja Rasâlu, tender-hearted and strong, journeyed along to play _chaupur_ with the King, he came to a burning forest, and a voice rose from the fire saying, 'O traveler, for God's sake, save me from the fire!'

Then the Prince turned towards the burning forest, and, lo! the voice was the voice of a tiny cricket. Nevertheless, Rasâlu, tender-hearted and strong, snatched it from the fire and set it at liberty. Then the little creature, full of gratitude, pulled out one of its feelers, and giving it to its preserver, said, 'Keep this, and should you ever be in trouble, put it into the fire, and instantly I will come to your aid.'

The Prince smiled, saying, 'What help could _you_ give _me_?' Nevertheless, he kept the hair and went on his way.

Now, when he reached the city of King Sarkap, seventy maidens, daughters of the King, came out to meet him-- seventy fair maidens, merry and careless, full of smiles and laughter; but one, the youngest of them all, when she saw the gallant young Prince riding on Bhaunr Irâqi, going gaily to his doom, was filled with pity, and called to him, saying--

'Fair Prince, on the charger so gray,
Turn thee back! turn thee back!
Or lower thy lance for the fray;
Thy head will be forfeit today!
Dost love life? then, stranger, I pray,
Turn thee back! turn thee back!'

But he, smiling at the maiden, answered lightly--

'Fair maiden, I come from afar,
Sworn conqueror in love and war!
King Sarkap my coming will rue,

His head in four pieces I'll hew;
Then forth as a bridegroom, I'll ride,
With you, little maid, as my bride!'

Now when Rasâlu replied so gallantly, the maiden looked in his face, and seeing how far he was, and how brave and strong, she straightway fell in love with him, and would gladly have followed him through the world.

But the other sixty-nine maidens, being jealous, laughed scornfully at her, saying, 'Not so fast, O gallant warrior! If you would marry our sister you must first do our bidding, for you will be our younger brother.'

'Fair sisters!' quoth Rasâlu gaily, 'give me my task and I will perform it.'

So the sixty-nine maidens mixed a hundredweight of millet seed with a hundredweight of sand, and giving it to Rasâlu, bade him separate the seed from the sand.

Then he bethought him of the cricket, and drawing the feeler from his pocket, thrust it into the fire. And immediately there was a whirring noise in the air, and a great flight of crickets alighted beside him, and among them the cricket whose life he had saved.

Then Rasâlu said, 'Separate the millet seed from the sand.'

'Is that all?' quoth the cricket; 'had I known how small a job you wanted me to do, I would not have assembled so many of my brethren.'

With that, the flight of crickets set to work, and in one night they separated the seed from the sand.

Now when the sixty-nine fair maidens, daughters of the King, saw that Rasâlu had performed his task, they set him another, bidding him swing them all, one by one, in their swings, until they were tired.

Whereupon he laughed, saying, 'There are seventy of you, counting my little bride yonder, and I am not going to spend my life in swinging girls; yet, by the time I have given each of you a swing, the first will be wanting another! No! if you want to swing, get in, all seventy of you, into one swing, and then I will see what I can compass.'

So the seventy maidens, merry and careless, full of smiles and laughter, climbed into the one swing, and Raja Rasâlu, standing in his shining armor, fastened the ropes to his mighty bow, and drew it up to its fullest bent. Then he let go, and like an arrow, the swing shot into the air, with its burden of seventy fair maidens, merry and careless, full of smiles and laughter.

But as it swung back again, Rasâlu, standing there in his shining armor, drew his sharp sword and severed the ropes. Then the seventy fair maidens fell to the ground headlong, and some were bruised and some broken, but the only one who escaped unhurt was the maiden who loved Rasâlu, for she fell out last, on the top of the others, and so came to no harm.

After this, Rasâlu strode on fifteen paces, till he came to the seventy drums, that everyone who came to play _chaupur_ with the King had to beat in turn; and he beat them so loudly that he broke them all. Then he came to the seventy gongs, all in a row, and he hammered them so hard that they cracked to pieces.

Seeing this, the youngest Princess, who was the only one who could run, fled to her father the King in a great fright, saying--

'A mighty Prince, Sarkar! making havoc rides along,
He swung us, seventy maidens fair, and threw us out headlong;
He broke the drums you placed there and the gongs too in

his pride,
Sure, he will kill thee, father mine, and take me for his bride!'

But King Sarkap replied scornfully--

'Silly maiden, thy words make a lot
Of a very small matter;
For fear of my valor, I wot,
His armor will clatter.
As soon as I've eaten my bread
I'll go forth and cut off his head!'

Notwithstanding these brave and boastful words, he was in reality very much afraid, having heard of Rasâlu's renown. And learning that he was stopping at the house of an old woman in the city, till the hour for playing _chaupur_ arrived, Sarkap sent slaves to him with trays of sweetmeats and fruit, as to an honored guest. But the food was poisoned.

Now when the slaves brought the trays to Raja Rasâlu, he rose haughtily, saying, 'Go, tell your master I have naught to do with him in friendship. I am his sworn enemy, and I eat not of his salt!'

So saying, he threw the sweetmeats to Raja Sarkap's dog, which had followed the slaves, and lo! the dog died.

Then Rasâlu was very wroth, and said bitterly, 'Go back to Sarkar, slaves! and tell him that Rasâlu deems it no act of bravery to kill even an enemy by treachery.'

HOW KING SARKAP AND RAJA RASLU PLAYED CHAUPUR.

Now, when evening came, Raja Rasâlu went forth to play _chaupur_ with King Sarkap, and as he passed some potters' kilns he saw a cat wandering about restlessly; so he asked what ailed her that she never stood still, and she replied, 'My kittens are in an unbaked pot in the kiln yonder. It has just been set alight, and my children will be baked alive; therefore I cannot rest!'

Her words moved the heart of Raja Rasâlu, and, going to the potter, he asked him to sell the kiln as it was; but the potter replied that he could not settle a fair price till the pots were burnt, as he could not tell how many would come out whole. Nevertheless, after some bargaining, he consented at last to sell the kiln, and Rasâlu, having searched through all the pots, restored the kittens to their mother, and she, in gratitude for his mercy, gave him one of them, saying, 'Put it in your pocket, for it will help you when you are in difficulties.'

So Raja Rasâlu put the kitten in his pocket and went to play _chaupur_ with the King.

Now, before they sat down to play, Raja Sarkap fixed his stakes. On the first game, his kingdom; on the second, the wealth of the whole world; and on the third, his head. So, likewise, Raja Rasâlu fixed his stakes. On the first game, his arms; on the second, his horse; and on the third, his head.

Then they began to play, and it fell to Rasâlu's lot to make the first move. Now he, forgetful of the dead man's warning, played with the dice given him by Raja Sarkar; then, in addition, Sarkar let loose his famous rat, Dhol Raja, and it ran about the board, upsetting the _chaupur_ pieces on the sly, so that Rasâlu lost the first game, and gave up his shining armor.

So the second game began, and once more Dhol Raja, the rat, upset the pieces; and Rasâlu, losing the game, gave up his faithful steed. Then Bhaunr Irâqi, who stood by, found a voice, and cried to his master--

'I am born of the sea and gold;
Dear Prince! trust me now as of old.
I'll carry you far from these wiles--

My flight, all spurred, will be swift as a bird,
For thousands and thousands of miles!
Or if needs you must stay; ere the next game you play,
Place hand in your pocket, I pray!'

Hearing this, Raja Sarkap frowned and bade his slaves remove Bhaunr Irâqi, since he gave his master advice in the game. Now when the slaves came to lead the faithful steed away, Rasâlu could not refrain from tears, thinking over the long years during which Bhaunr Irâqi had been his companion. But the horse cried out again--

'Weep not, dear Prince! I shall not eat my bread
Of stranger's hands, nor to strange stall be led.
Take thy right hand, and place it as I said.'

These words roused some recollection in Rasâlu's mind, and when, just at this moment, the kitten in his pocket began to struggle, he remembered the warning that the corpse had given him about the dice made from dead men's bones. Then his heart rose once more, and he called boldly to Raja Sarkar, 'Leave my horse and arms here for the present. Time enough to take them away when you have won my head!'

Now, Raja Sarkar, seeing Rasâlu's confident bearing, began to be afraid, and ordered all the women of his palace to come forth in their gayest attire and stand before Rasâlu, to distract his attention from the game. But he never even looked at them, and drawing the dice from his pocket, said to Sarkar, 'We have played with your dice all this time; now we will play with mine.'

Then the kitten went and sat at the window through which the rat Dhol Raja used to come, and the game began.

After a while, Sarkar, seeing Raja Rasâlu was winning, called to his rat, but when Dhol Raja saw the kitten he was afraid, and would not go farther. So Rasâlu won and took back his arms. Next, he played for his horse, and once more Raja Sarkap called for his rat; but Dhol Raja, seeing the kitten keeping watch, was afraid. So Rasâlu won the second stake and took back Bhaunr Irâqi.

Then Sarkar brought all his skill to bear on the third and last game, saying--

'O molded pieces, favor me today!
For smooth, this is a man with whom I play.
No paltry risk--but life and death at stake;
As Sarkap does, so do, for Sarkap's sake!'

But Rasâlu answered back--

'O molded pieces, favor me today!
For smooth, it is a man with whom I play.
No paltry risk--but life and death at stake;
As Heaven does, so do, for Heaven's sake!'

So they began to play, whilst the women stood round in a circle, and the kitten watched Dhol Raja from the window. Then Sarkar lost, first his kingdom, then the wealth of the whole world, and lastly his head.

Just then, a servant came in to announce the birth of a daughter to Raja Sarkar, and he, overcome by misfortunes, said, 'Kill her at once! for she has been born in an evil moment and has brought her father ill luck!'

But Rasâlu rose in his shining armor, tenderhearted and strong, saying, 'Not so, O king! She has done no evil. Give me this child to wife; and if you will vow, by all you hold sacred, never again to play _chaupur_ for another's head, I will spare yours now!'

Then Sarkar vowed a solemn vow never to play for another's head; and after that, he took a fresh mango branch, and the newborn babe, and placing them on a golden dish, gave them to the Prince.

Now, as Rasâlu left the palace, carrying with him the new-born babe and the mango branch, he met a band of prisoners, and they called out to him--

'A royal hawk art thou, O King! the rest
But timid wild fowl. Grant us our request--
Unloose these chains, and live forever blest!'

And Raja Rasâlu hearkened to them and bade King Sarkap set them at liberty.

Then he went to the Murti Hills, placed the newborn babe¦ Kokilan, in an underground palace, and planted the mango branch at the door, saying, 'In twelve years the mango tree will blossom; then will I return and marry Kokilan.'

And after twelve years, the mango tree began to flower, and Raja Rasâlu married Princess Kokilan, whom he won from Sarkap when he played _chaupur_ with the King.